Claws

Written by Carol Krueger

Look at the claws
on these animals.
Animals can use their claws
in lots of different ways.

This cat is using
its claws to climb.
It could use its claws
to scratch and fight, too.

claw

paw

The cat can pull its claws
inside its paws.
It can keep its claws safe.

5

Some animals use
their claws to get food.
This bear is using
its claws to get berries.

6

crab

coconut

This crab is using
its sharp claws to open
a coconut.

7

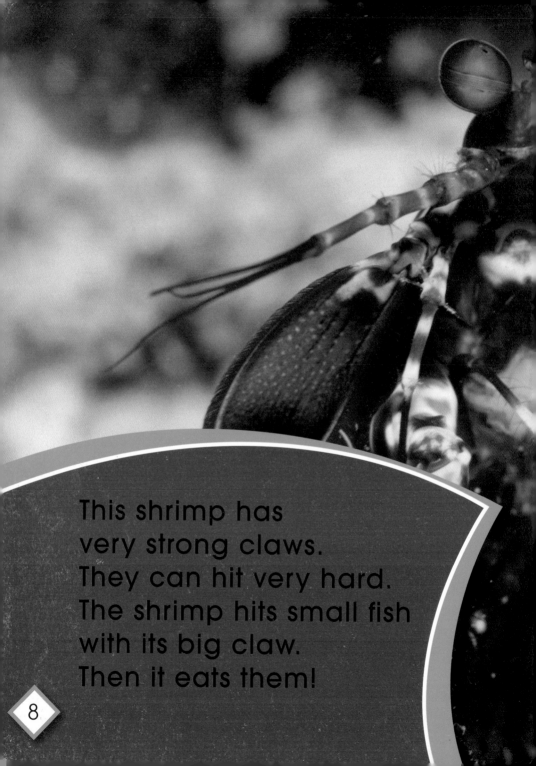

This shrimp has
very strong claws.
They can hit very hard.
The shrimp hits small fish
with its big claw.
Then it eats them!

big claw

hair

This animal is called a head louse.

claw

This very small animal
lives in hair.
It has small claws that
help it hold on to the hair.

10

food

claw

This eagle has big claws.
It can use its claws
to carry food
when it is flying.

This skunk has sharp claws. It can use its claws for digging in the ground.

This wolf uses its claws
to dig, too.
It can hide some food.
When it is hungry, it will
dig the food up again.

13

This crab is waving
its big claw.
It is telling other crabs
to stay away!

Index

◾◾◾ **Guide Notes**

Title: Claws
Stage: Early (4) – Green

Genre: Nonfiction
Approach: Guided Reading
Processes: Thinking Critically, Exploring Language, Processing Information
Written and Visual Focus: Photographs (static images), Labels, Index

THINKING CRITICALLY
(sample questions)
- Look at the front cover and the title. Ask the children what they know about animals' claws.
- Look at the title and read it to the children.
- Focus the children's attention on the index. Ask: "What are you going to find out about in this book?"
- If you want to find out about a crab's claws, what pages would you look on?
- If you want to find out about a wolf's claws, what page would you look on?
- Look at page 6. How else do you think the bear could get berries?
- Look at page 10. Why do you think the head lice need to hold on to people's hair?

EXPLORING LANGUAGE

Terminology
Title, cover, photographs, author, photographers

Vocabulary
Interest words: claws, paws, berries, coconut, shrimp, eagle, skunk, wolf
High-frequency words: could, keep
Positional words: inside, on, in, up

Print Conventions
Capital letter for sentence beginnings, periods, commas, exclamation marks